TEENAGE READING

THE TIME DETECTIVES

THE DISAPPEARANCE OF
DANNY
DOYLE

**FICTION
EXPRESS**

What do other readers think?

Here are some comments left on the Fiction Express blog about the book:

"I am officially hooked with this book! Alex Woolf is a really talented writer!"
Sophia, Woking

"I didn't want the book to end!"
Isra, Coventry

"This is a phenomenal book, it has helped me in my reading and writing."
Liberty D, Bristol

"Your books are amazing, I love them lots!"
James, Telford

"My class is hooked by The Disappearance of Danny Doyle.*"*
Jayne Fisher, Flint High School

"Hi Alex, I love your book because I love mysteries and adventure novels!"
Lainey, North Yorkshire

"I love this book because it is really interesting the way that they went back in time!"
Henna, Birmingham

Contents

I would like to thank all the wonderful children who took the time to read this story and cast their votes on the Fiction Express website. Without your contribution, this book could not have been written. I would also like to thank Laura Durman, Paul Humphrey and Gill Humphrey at Fiction Express for their invaluable advice, support and editorial comments during the writing process.

Chapter 1

The Missing Twin

"Come on, cuz! Let's go in."

Without waiting for Joe to answer, Maya pushed open the door and entered the old, tumbledown house. The hallway was dim, the air stuffy and filled with tiny specks of dust that sparkled as they floated through the sunlight streaming in from behind her. A rickety-looking staircase curved upwards into shadow.

"We should leave," said Joe, still loitering at the doorway. "There might be someone living here."

"No way!" said Maya. "Who would live in an old dump like this in the middle of a wood?" She turned and stared at him accusingly. "I can't believe I've been down here in deepest, darkest Dorset for two whole weeks, bored out of my mind, and only now do you think to show me this place."

Joe looked deflated, and Maya thought she might have been a bit hard on him. She grinned and did a twirl, making the floorboards creak beneath her. "Better late than never, though, eh? It's wicked, Joe!"

Joe eyed the rickety staircase anxiously. "It looks dangerous to me."

"Come on!" she cried, and flew up the stairs, taking them three at a time. The ancient timbers groaned and shifted under her weight, but she was too excited to notice. She came to a crooked passageway with doors leading off it. She stopped, the smile fading from her face. Was that a door closing at the far end?

It was probably just the wind.

"Come on up, cuz!" she yelled at Joe.

He eventually arrived, having climbed the stairs much more carefully.

Maya led the way down the passage, deciding not to mention the closing door – she didn't want to scare Joe off just after finally tempting him in.

Opening a door on her left, she found a room piled high with very old cardboard boxes. Some of them were so full, or so squashed by those stacked above them, that they had split. Papers, yellow with age, were spilling on to the floor. Maya picked one up. It was a copy of a letter, dated 1st May 1956, addressed to someone in Dorsetshire County Council and signed Michael Doyle. He was asking if they had any information about his twin brother, a "missing evacuee" called Daniel Doyle.

Maya glanced up, her skin prickling. Was someone watching them?

No, it was just this house, giving her the creeps! She picked up another letter. It was addressed to the same official and was another enquiry from Michael Doyle about his missing brother, this time dated 1st June 1956.

"Michael Doyle, Daniel Doyle," muttered Joe, who was leafing through another pile of papers on the far side of the room. "Do you think they used to live here?"

Her curiosity now aroused, Maya picked up a whole sheaf of letters from the floor and began going through them. They were all virtually the same, except for the dates, which were always one month apart. She stared again at the papers scattered about her feet like autumn leaves, and then at the mountain of boxes piled up in front of her. "OMG!" she said. "This guy must have spent his whole life searching for his brother."

"What was that?" said Joe suddenly.

"I said this guy must have–"

"Shhh!" hissed Joe, glancing anxiously at the door. "I heard a noise outside."

"Probably a rat," said Maya, shivering slightly.

"Let's get out of here," said Joe.

But Maya wasn't ready to leave yet. These letters, the sheer number of them, in this abandoned old house – it was creepy, yet so intriguing!

Suddenly, they heard a thundering outside, as if someone in heavy boots was approaching. Maya and Joe went rigid with fright. There was nowhere to run. The boxes were blocking access to any window.

They both jumped as the door flew open. Staring down at them was an old man – a very old man – with bright blue eyes starting from his head. In his shaking hands was a shotgun, the muzzle pointing at Maya and Joe.

"What are you doing in here?" he demanded. "Get out of my house before I shoot the pair of you!"

Maya could see that the man was almost as scared as they were. And, by the way he was shaking, he was unlikely to hit either of them, except by accident. She swallowed and forced herself to be brave. "Hi," she said as calmly and cheerfully as she could manage. "I'm Maya. This is Joe. We're sorry if we've broken into your house. We didn't think anyone lived here."

The old man shouldered the weapon and took a more careful aim at Joe. "If you two snoopers aren't out of here by the time I count to five, I'll fire. I'm within my rights you know. I could shoot you both! He looked like he meant it. "One…!" he shouted. "Two…!"

Joe made for the door.

"Three…!" bellowed the man.

"Come on!" Joe shouted desperately at Maya. But she didn't move. There was something about this man. It wasn't just fear and rage she could see in his eyes, but a whole world of sadness. She knew then that he was Michael Doyle, the writer of all these letters. Maybe they could help him, if they could just…

"Four…!"

"Wait!" shouted Maya. "We can help you find your brother!"

The old man blinked and lowered his weapon. Then he took aim again. "What can a pair of kids like you do?"

Maya sensed Joe staring at her wide-eyed. She knew he was probably quietly freaking out, but she couldn't stop now. "We can find your brother, Mr Doyle," she said. "Trust us! We really can!"

The old man's anger flickered and died, and the creases around his eyes formed into lines of sadness. They seemed to be the natural contours of his face. The gun muzzle sagged towards the floor as his eyes roamed the mountain range of boxes in the room. "I've spent my whole life looking for him," he said. "I've written to every government department, every evacuee organization. I've put messages in the newspapers, on the Internet. It's like he never existed…" Michael Doyle's lips trembled with long-nurtured resentment.

"But he did exist! We were both evacuated here, as youngsters, in 1940."

He slowly sank down on to a box, lost in his memories. "We were glad to get away from London – Danny especially. He'd always had a sense of adventure that kid. Reckless some called him. I was quieter, more cautious…."

His voice trailed away as he choked back a tear.

"Go on, Mr Doyle," urged Maya gently.

The old man pulled himself together and continued.

"Our lives until then had been miserable. Dad was ill most of the time and couldn't get a job. We hardly had enough money for food – didn't even have a bed to sleep in. We'd never seen the countryside before we came to Dorset. A very happy year we had in Charlton Abbas. Well, apart from that business with Simon Kellaway…."

"Simon Kellaway?" exclaimed Joe. Charlton Abbas was his home village, and he knew the Kellaways. They were still a rough bunch.

"Yes, a big old bully he was, and he had it in for Danny.

But apart from him, it was great – best time of our lives – that is until the night Danny disappeared."

Maya glanced at Joe, who was listening intently to the old man.

"I don't suppose either of you are twins," said Michael. "It's hard to explain. It's not like losing a brother – more like losing part of yourself. I've never been right since I lost Danny." He pulled a grubby handkerchief from his pocket and dabbed his eyes.

"I'm sorry," murmured Joe.

"I just wish I knew where he went to that night and why he never came back."

"Didn't the police try and find him?" Joe asked.

"For a bit," replied Michael. "But this was wartime, remember. They had more important things to worry about."

Maya was glad to see that Joe was as hooked as she was by Michael's story. She noticed Joe's hand had slid into the pocket where he kept his timephone – the device they could use to travel back into history. Joe must have been thinking the same thing she was. They hadn't used the phone since the previous summer when they'd gone back to 1840 to solve the mystery of Maddie Musgrove, the young maidservant hanged for stealing her mistress's jewellery. Maya hoped the phone still worked.

"When exactly did Danny disappear?" Joe asked.

"The 19th of April 1941," said Michael. "The date is engraved in my memory. The last time I saw him was that afternoon. He told me he was on his way to a warehouse near Beaminster. Danny had got himself a job with a local businessman, a dodgy fellow named Dawkins – I just thought it must be something to do with that. Then, at about half past six that evening, Mrs Morrison – she was the village postwoman – she was driving back from the sorting office in Bridport with some deliveries when she said she saw Danny running through Vipers' Fold, that very field out there."

The children turned and looked through the dirty window into the meadow beyond.

"Someone was chasing him, so she said, but she couldn't make out who. She told the police it looked like just a children's game and so she thought no more of it. As far as I know, she was the last person to see my brother."

Maya and Joe exchanged glances. They both knew what they wanted to do, but how do they explain it to Michael?

"Mr Doyle," said Maya, "we think we can help you."

"Do you have a photo of the two of you? I mean from the time you were evacuees?" Joe asked.

Michael rifled through one of the boxes and eventually handed Joe a tatty old photo. "Taken in 1941," he said, "just a few weeks before Danny disappeared."

The faded black and white image showed two curly-haired boys standing side by side in the front garden of a cottage. One was grinning cheekily, the other looking more serious. Apart from that, they were uncannily alike.

"Mind you, that was taken after a year eating decent country food. You should have seen us when we first arrived. Dirty street urchins we were, thin as sticks."

"Well, thank you, Mr Doyle," said Joe, handing the photo back. "I think we have all we need." He ushered Maya towards the door.

"Hang on a minute," said Michael. "What are you planning to–?"

"You'll see," said Joe with a grin.

Chapter 2

Evacuees

Joe and Maya left the old man standing among his memories, a puzzled expression on his face. Outside the house, they walked a short way through the woods, along the lane that led to Charlton Abbas.

Joe looked back towards the house, still just visible through the thick trees. "We should be out of sight here," he said, taking out his timephone. It immediately lit up, with the words:

**Hello Joe Smallwood.
Which time would you like to visit?**

"Let's head back to the 17th of April 1941, two days before Danny disappeared," said Joe. "That'll give us time to check out any suspects. Are you ready?"

"I'm ready," said Maya, taking his hand.

She watched as Joe twirled the date wheels on the phone's screen, taking them back through the months and years.

The scene around them shimmered and faded. Quicker than expected, the surrounding woods came back into focus, but the trees looked younger and more sparse. Michael's house could now be clearly seen through their slender branches. It looked in a much better state than the one they had left minutes before. Fresh green ivy grew on its walls, and its brown roof tiles were now unbroken and free of moss.

Maya was not new to time travel, but it always gave her a thrill. She squeezed Joe's hand. "We've done it!"

Her clothes felt different. She looked down and saw that instead of the jeans and tee shirt she'd put on that morning, she was wearing a neatly buttoned coat over a blouse and skirt, with white socks and heavy black shoes. Joe was looking uncomfortable in shorts, a blue shirt buttoned to his neck and a sleeveless grey jumper. An old-fashioned raincoat was draped over this arm.

As they stood there absorbing all these changes, the door of the house opened and an old lady stepped out into the small front garden. Her long grey and black hair hung loose down to her shoulders. She glanced up and stared at Joe and Maya, her sharp nose twitching. Then she smiled.

"Ah! There you are, children," she said in a high, rasping voice. "You made it at last. Come in now. There's so much to be done."

Joe and Maya stared at each other in shock. How could this woman have known they were about to appear?

Before they could react, they heard the rattle of a

bicycle chain behind them, and a squeak of brakes. They turned to see a large woman dressed in a uniform of blue cap and matching jacket, tie and skirt, balanced precariously on a heavy black bicycle. She wobbled to a halt in front of them.

"More evacuees!" she boomed in an exasperated tone. "You keep turning up, don't you? Where's your luggage and gas masks?"

"Er…." began Joe.

"Never mind!" the woman retorted. "You'd better come back to the village with me and I'll see if I can sort out some lodging for you. I'm Mrs Morrison, by the way – postmistress and official evacuee billeting officer for Charlton Abbas."

As Mrs Morrison was turning her bicycle around, she was arrested by an outraged cry from the old lady in the front garden. "I'll have you know that those children are mine," she screeched. "I've been expecting them."

Mrs Morrison clearly didn't like being argued with. She drew herself to her full, considerable height and bellowed back: "Winifred Coombes, as you very well know you've been declared unfit to host evacuees. The children are coming back with me."

"You only said I was unfit because you don't like me," the old lady spat back. "None of you lot in the village like me." She turned to the children and her sharp face broke into a thin-lipped smile. "And, anyway, you've come here to work for me, haven't you dears? Come now. Don't be shy." She held open the door for them.

"They're coming with me, Winifred," roared Mrs Morrison, her face now pink with fury.

As the two women argued, Maya whispered to Joe: "I don't like the look of either of them, do you?"

"Not much," he shuddered. "That old lady gives me the creeps. I think we'd be safer going with Mrs Morrison. She seems such a busybody, she'll know everything that's going on in the village. We're sure to get some useful info from her. And, don't forget, she was the last person to see Danny."

Maya shook her head. "I reckon we'll be better off staying with Winnie the Witch. Her house backs on to Vipers' Fold, where Danny was last seen. We'll be able to keep an eye on it if we stay there. Who knows, the old lady might even be involved in his disappearance."

Joe seemed unsure. "Maybe we shouldn't go with either of them," he suggested suddenly. "What about if we tell them we're on our way home to Braden Hill? That's another village near here. Then we could camp out in the woods and try and find the Doyle brothers tomorrow."

Maya looked at him doubtfully.

"I've camped in these woods before," he reassured her, showing her the Swiss Army knife he had in his pocket.

"What are you going to do with that?" she giggled, "Skin a rabbit?"

Joe shrugged his shoulders. "What do you think we should we do then?" he asked.

Chapter 3

The Bully

Maya was silent for a moment, weighing up the options.

"Let's do it!" she grinned. "Let's camp out in the woods! That way we'll be free to move around as we please and spy on whoever we want."

Smiling, Joe agreed.

Meanwhile, the argument between the women was continuing at full throttle.

"Of course people don't trust you, Winifred," bellowed Mrs Morrison loudly enough to scare the birds in the trees. "You keep yourself hidden away in this house. And I'm not one to listen to gossip, but there have been rumours of some very odd activity late at night. Torchlight seen in your back garden, in defiance of the blackout! What are people supposed to think?"

"Excuse me," Joe timidly interjected. "I think there's been some sort of misunderstanding. You see, we actually live in Braden Hill. We were just on our way back there, in fact."

The two women stared at him. "Well, you might have said!" declared Mrs Morrison indignantly, adjusting her cap and climbing on to her bike.

After the postmistress had wobbled off down the path, Winifred Coombes smiled at them and said: "You are the children, aren't you? The ones I was expecting?"

"Er, no," said Joe, backing away and tugging at Maya's sleeve. "We really aren't!"

With that, both children turned and ran as fast as they could back along the path leading deeper into the wood. When they'd reached a safe distance, Maya stopped Joe and laughed breathlessly: "I'm so glad we got away from them, aren't you?" She breathed the sweet air of the forest.

"Before we make our camp, why don't we sneak into the village and see what we can find out?" suggested Joe.

"But Mrs Morrison might see us," Maya pointed out.

"Not if we take the back way in. Follow me."

Joe led her on a circuitous route, through a dense, trackless part of the forest, into a meadow and then on to a narrow road bordered by high hedges. "This'll be a dual carriageway one day," he commented.

Twenty minutes later, they were standing on Charlton Abbas High Street.

"Hey," marvelled Joe. "Our Chinese takeaway has become a greengrocer!" The range of produce on display looked poor – lettuce, beans, potatoes, stumpy carrots, greenish tomatoes, rhubarb.

As they stood there, a boy suddenly burst out of the village shop next door, carrying a big glass jar of sweets, and ran down the street. Maya recognized him immediately.

"That was Danny," she said, before frowning. "… Or maybe Michael."

A man in an apron charged out after the boy, crying "Stop, thief!"

"Whoaa!" gasped Maya. "Come on, let's try and catch him up."

Joe tugged her in another direction. "I know where he'll probably hide out," he said, beckoning her towards a narrow passage between a bakery and a pub.

They ran through the cobbled alleyway, strewn with barrels and sacks of waste. They found the thief in a little doorway, cheeks flushed, breathing hard.

He looked up at them in alarm. In the street at the end of the alley, they saw the shopkeeper rush by, still searching for him.

"Please don't give me away," whispered the boy.

"Give me one good reason why we shouldn't, Danny Doyle!" demanded Maya fiercely.

The boy stared up at her in surprise. Then he swallowed and said: "I'm Michael actually. And I'm only stealing these sweets because Simon Kellaway forced me to. He's waiting in his hideout in the woods, and if I don't bring them to him straight away, he'll beat up Danny. He's holding him hostage there."

"Then let's go to the police," said Joe. "This should be reported."

"Do me a favour!" said Michael. "Kellaway's dad's the local copper. He won't believe us against his son."

"Then we'll go with you to Simon Kellaway and force him to let Danny go," said Maya.

Michael looked at them and shook his head sadly. "You don't know Simon then. He's only fifteen, but he's as big and strong as a man. He's got his mates with him, too. We wouldn't stand a chance."

Maya glanced at Joe, who muttered: "I still think we should call the police."

"Come on!" said Maya, picking up the jar of sweets. "Let's take these back first."

Michael looked worried by this plan, but didn't stop her.

The shop was empty when they got there. Michael was just replacing the jar on the shelf behind the counter when the shopkeeper arrived, looking puffed and angry.

"Michael Doyle! It is Michael, isn't it? I'm surprised at you, young man! I know sweets are rationed, but that's no reason to start stealing them."

"I'm really sorry, Mr Watkins," whimpered Michael. "Simon Kellaway made me do it." He explained the situation, and Mr Watkins calmed down, muttering that something really needed to be done about "that Kellaway boy".

A customer entered, and Mr Watkins went to serve her. Michael said to Joe and Maya: "How will we get Danny back now?"

"We'll go and talk to Simon," said Maya. "I'm sure we can make him see reason."

"You *definitely* don't know him then," said Michael.

"Are you sure about this, Maya?" queried Joe.

Maya took him aside and whispered: "Kellaway has to be one of our chief suspects. We need to check him out."

Joe thought for a moment. Then his face suddenly brightened. "I've got an idea." He turned to Mr Watkins, who had now finished serving the customer. "Excuse me," said Joe. "Do you sell string by any chance?"

"We certainly do, young man." He went to fetch some from a shelf at the back of the shop.

"What are you going to do with string?" asked Maya. "Challenge Kellaway to a game of conkers?"

"I'm going to make a bow and arrow," announced Joe.

Maya rolled her eyes at Michael. "He must reckon he's Bear Grylls or something."

"Who?" frowned Michael.

"Never mind!" She turned back to Joe. "How about we also stock up on some food while we're here. And maybe a blanket."

"Good idea," agreed Joe.

Soon, Mr Watkins had prepared them a couple of brown paper bags full of the supplies they had asked for. Joe took out some money to pay him with, then stopped and stared at it, baffled.

"My mum gave me ten pounds this morning," he exclaimed. "Now look at it!"

Mr Watkins laughed. "Ten pounds! Who's your mum then, the Duchess of Devonshire? Here, let me look at that."

Joe handed him the note.

"That's a ten bob note, son," chuckled the shopkeeper.

"A what?"

"Ten shillings," explained the shopkeeper. "More than enough to pay for this lot."

Soon, the three of them were walking back towards the wood that encircled much of the village.

"Who exactly are you people?" Michael asked as they walked.

"I'm Joe, and this is Maya," said Joe.

"How do you know Danny?"

"We don't know him," said Maya quickly. "We've heard of him because he knows Mr, um…." She wracked her brains trying to remember the name of the 'dodgy businessman' Michael's older version had mentioned. "…Mr Dawkins?"

Michael nodded ruefully. "I've been warning him to steer clear of that man," he said. "Our foster mum, Mrs Welbridge, 'Auntie Vi' we call her, she says Jack Dawkins is a spiv. He dresses smart and talks in this way that makes you want to believe everything he says. But Auntie Vi says it's all a pack of lies. The things he sells are stolen, or else they're black market stuff. You know, like rationed food or clothes. Danny swears he's legit, but I've got my doubts."

* * *

Back in the wood, Joe quickly found a suitable tree on which to build their shelter. The tree had a fork about a metre off the ground, and into this he placed the end of a long branch, which he called the ridgepole.

"We're camping out for the night," Maya explained to Michael.

They helped Joe create walls out of smaller sticks and

dead leaves, leaving a gap for the entrance. Then Joe got to work making his bow and arrow. Maya and Michael watched, bemused, as he picked up sticks, examining them, then discarding them. Finally, he found one he was satisfied with.

"Yew wood," said Joe. "Nice and bendy." He took out his penknife and began shaving off some of the wood from each end, so the thickest part was in the centre. Then he cut notches to hold the bow string. Before long, he had made himself an impressive-looking bow. All that remained was to whittle himself a set of arrows.

Chapter 4

Encounter in the Forest

The light in the forest had turned the deep gold of late afternoon by the time a reluctant Michael led Joe and Maya to Kellaway's hideout. The boy was clearly scared out of his wits, and it had taken all Maya's persuasive powers to get him to agree to their strategy.

"He'll kill us," he muttered as they walked. "He'll string us up from the highest tree and pelt us with stones."

"Not me," said Maya, defiantly.

They were walking along a narrow track when Michael stopped suddenly and pulled Maya behind a tree.

"Quick, hide!" he hissed at Joe.

Joe ducked behind a bush.

"That's Neville Groat up ahead," whispered Michael. "He's one of Kellaway's gang."

Maya peered down the path and saw, not twenty metres away, a scruffy-looking boy lying on the grass, idly tossing pebbles into a shallow stream.

As she watched, the drooping branches of the willow

tree behind him suddenly twitched, and a much bigger boy emerged. His red hair was shorn close to his scalp. He had pale skin, thick red lips and a prominent forehead that looked set in a frown of permanent anger.

"Th-that's Simon," stammered a terrified Michael.

"Oi!" Simon Kellaway shouted at young Neville, giving him a kick. "You're supposed to be on guard duty! Get up!"

The boy clambered to his feet.

Kellaway parted the curtain of willow branches and nodded to someone within. A blond-haired kid emerged, dragging another, smaller boy behind him. It was Danny, and he was the spitting image of Michael, except for the bruise on his cheek and the defiant look in his eye.

Kellaway shoved him in the chest, making Danny totter backwards. "Your brother never showed up," the bully snarled. "That's very bad news for you, Danny boy!" He picked him up by the collar, so his feet dangled in the air. "What's it to be then? Do you want us to dunk you in the river and then beat you up, or do you want to get beaten up first and then dunked? Your choice."

He cackled at his mates and they chortled back.

"Do what you like, Kellaway," spat Danny.

"How many of them are there?" Joe whispered to Michael.

"Just three," murmured Michael. "But Simon's worth at least two by himself."

Joe quietly placed an arrow in his bow and took aim down the path.

Maya noticed he was sweating and biting his lip.

"I-I'll fire a warning shot," he rasped.

The bowstring was pulled taut, the arrow head trembling, but he didn't fire.

"Do it, Joe," Maya urged.

"What do you reckon, boys?" Kellaway was smirking. "Let's dunk him first, shall we?"

"Yeah, chuck him in!" laughed the blond boy.

There was a big splash as Danny was hurled into the shallow water. At that moment, Joe's arrow whistled along the path and lodged with a thwack in a tree trunk about a metre above Neville Groat's head.

The boy let out a shout of terror.

"What was that?"

Kellaway and his sidekicks stared down the path as Maya shouted in as bold a voice as she could manage: "Let the boy go, Kellaway! Or the next one will be aimed at your head!"

There was a sudden flurry of movement from the stream. A very wet Danny sprang up and pushed the blond boy over, then dashed off into the forest.

"After him!" screamed Kellaway, and his friends took off, crashing through the undergrowth.

Kellaway continued to stare down the path. "Who's there?" he grunted. "That you, Mikey? Brought your girlfriend, have you?"

Maya didn't reply, preferring to make him sweat.

All at once, Kellaway charged like a bull.

Michael emitted a shriek of fear, and bolted, quickly followed by Joe and Maya.

They ran as fast as they could through the trees, but Kellaway always seemed to be just behind them, his feet thudding on the ground like pounding hammers, his breath like a steam train in their ears.

Michael scrambled over a fence and raced into the meadow beyond. Maya and Joe leapt after him, falling briefly to their knees, before lumbering forwards through the long grass. They ran a further hundred metres before realizing that Kellaway was no longer behind them. Maya glanced around and stopped, surprised. She saw him standing by the fence, his fists clenched in frustrated rage. "I'll get you next time, Michael Doyle!" he bawled. "You just wait! I'll tear you limb from limb! And that brother of yours."

Michael, Joe and Maya collapsed to the ground, fighting to get their breath back. As they lay there, another figure came sprinting over to them. Danny fell down in a sodden heap, laughing so hard he couldn't speak.

In the distance, Maya saw his pursuers standing helplessly at the fence next to Kellaway. The bullies stared at them for a moment before turning and melting back into the wood.

"Thank you," gasped Danny. "Thank you, my friends!"

Michael made the introductions.

"Pleased to meet you, Joe and Maya," said Danny, standing up and giving them a bow. "Or should I call you Robin Hood and Maid Marian?"

Maya laughed at this.

"Why didn't they follow us in here?" Joe wanted to know.

"This place is our only refuge from them," said Michael.

"They'll never come into this field," said Danny. "Kellaway was bitten by a snake here once, when he was little. Nearly killed him, it did."

"I wish it had," Michael muttered.

"He's been scared to come here ever since," Danny went on. "It's out of bounds to his mates, too. He doesn't want them looking braver than him."

Suddenly Maya realized where they were. At the far end of the field was the back of Winifred Coombes' house. "This is Vipers' Fold, isn't it?" she said.

"Certainly is," sighed Danny, leaning back and relishing the cool evening breeze on his face. "And if I ever find the snake that bit Simon Kellaway, I'll give it a big fat kiss!"

* * *

A short while later, Maya and Joe said goodbye to the Doyle brothers, then returned to their little camp in the woods. After a meal of bread and cold beans, they lay next to each other on the soft bedding of leaves and looked up through the tree branches at the stars.

Maya was thinking about what Danny had said to them earlier. "So it couldn't have been Kellaway or his mates that Mrs Morrison saw running after Danny through Vipers' Fold," she said.

"No," agreed Joe. "So who was it then?"

They were pondering this mystery when a bright light suddenly flickered across the clearing next to their camp.

Maya grabbed Joe's arm in fright. "What was that?" she whispered.

"Don't know," croaked Joe, trembling.

Quietly, Maya sat up. The leaves rustled loudly beneath her. Dazzling torchlight flared in her eyes, and she quickly dropped back close to the ground.

"Stay absolutely still." she breathed in Joe's ear.

When the light didn't return, Maya hesitantly raised her head again. About a hundred metres away, she saw a torch beam, bobbing and flickering through the trees. "What's over there?" she asked, pointing.

"That's the path leading from the village," Joe said. "I wonder who it could be at this time of night."

"Let's go and find out," said Maya, jumping up.

They followed a course parallel to the path, keeping about ten metres inside the wood, crouching as they went and trying to avoid stepping on twigs. The moon was bright, illuminating the path quite clearly. They saw two figures. The one holding the torch was a tall, lean man in a pork pie hat and double-breasted suit. He was murmuring in a low voice as they walked. Maya saw he had a thin moustache and quite a charming smile. The other, smaller figure, was Danny Doyle.

"Dawkins," Joe whispered.

They followed Danny and his companion as they rounded a bend.

Ahead of them lay Winifred Coombes' house.

"Why would they be going to see the witch?" wondered Maya.

But they weren't. Danny and Dawkins walked right on past Winifred's house and continued along the path.

Maya and Joe were forced to move away from the path to get around the cottage. They were passing through the gap between her back garden and Vipers' Fold when Joe suddenly stopped.

"What is it?" hissed Maya. "We'll lose them if we don't hurry."

"Look!" said Joe, pointing at the back garden.

Maya stared in surprise. Winifred Coombes was digging a hole waist deep in the middle of her vegetable patch.

"What's she doing digging a hole in her garden at midnight?" gasped Maya. "Doesn't anybody go to bed around here?"

"We have to check this out," said Joe.

"But what about Danny and Dawkins? We'll lose them if we hang around here."

They stared at each other, wondering what to do.

"We'll just have to split up," suggested Maya. "You stay here and keep watch on Winnie while I follow Danny and Dawkins. We'll meet back at the camp later and compare notes."

Joe looked at her. "Are you sure? What if one of us gets caught or something?"

Chapter 5

Suspicious Goings on

Maya started down the track, anxious not to lose her quarry. The light from Jack Dawkins' torch was now just a faint glimmer up ahead, and she broke into a run to catch up with them. A light rain had started to fall. It hissed on the leaves, muffling the sound of her footsteps as she moved through the trees. She edged closer, trying to catch what Dawkins was saying to Danny.

"I think it's time you stepped up a level, Danny boy," Dawkins muttered, pulling up the collar of his jacket to protect himself from the rain. "Call it a promotion, my son. You've proved yourself a first-class salesman. Now it's time I introduced you to, ahem… to the other side of my business."

"You mean like where you buy stuff from, Mr Dawkins."

Dawkins laughed loudly at this, as if Danny had just said something extremely funny. "*Buy stuff from*! I like it, Danny!" he chuckled, guiding the boy off the main path and on to a grassy track. Maya hesitated a moment, then shot across the path and followed them on to the track. It was deeply rutted, as if regularly used by a car or van.

The trees grew thickly on either side, shrouding the track in darkness, and Maya could see nothing apart from the yellow torch beam ahead. Eventually they rounded a bend and came to a clearing, in the middle of which was a large brick garage. Its double doors stood ajar, and a light gleamed from within. Dawkins opened the doors wider. He ushered Danny inside, but didn't shut the doors behind him.

Maya tiptoed closer and crouched down behind one of the doors, keeping out of sight of those inside. She bent her head close to try and catch what they were saying, hardly daring to breathe in case she was discovered.

* * *

Joe wished he had his hoody on and not this old-fashioned raincoat, which didn't seem to be waterproof at all. The cold rain had begun trickling down his neck and seeping through his clothes. He also wished he'd stopped Maya from running off like that. Spying on a witch at midnight while getting soaked to the skin was bad enough. Doing it on your own was worse. He watched as Winnie, her long hair hanging down like strands of wet seaweed, climbed out of the hole she'd dug in her vegetable patch. She stretched a tarpaulin cover over it and weighed this down with some bricks. Then she used her shovel to scatter a thin layer of earth

34

over the tarpaulin, so that no one would ever know a hole had been dug there. After that, she made her way across the garden to the back door of her house.

So she'd dug a secret hole.

Big deal!

Joe could picture Maya's disappointed face when he told her. He had to find out more – like why she'd done it.

* * *

Maya barely noticed the rain pattering down, gradually soaking her hair and clothes. From inside the garage, she heard Dawkins speaking:

"Well, hello there Eric, old chum,' he said in his charming way. "So pleased you could make it. This here is my young… eh, apprentice, Daniel Doyle."

"You never told me you were bringing anyone else, Jack," came a gruff, slightly threatening voice. "You know I don't like surprises."

"Fear not, my friend," Dawkins answered smoothly. "Master Doyle has my utmost confidence. Danny, meet Eric Swinburn, security guard at Harrison's Warehouse, near Beaminster."

"Pleased to meet you, Mr Swinburn, sir," said Danny.

"Right, let's get down to business," said Dawkins. "Is everything still okay for the 19th, Eric?"

"Uh huh," grunted Eric

"It's a Saturday, so the warehouse will be closed, right?"

"Right."

"And the only person there will be you, right?" asked Dawkins.

"Right, just me and Tony."

"Tony?" Dawkins suddenly sounded worried.

"Yeah, my workmate, Tony," said Eric. "But he won't be there at four o'clock when you show up."

"How do you know that?" demanded Dawkins.

"Let's just say I've made arrangements," said Eric mysteriously. "Tony will be indisposed."

"Nice one, Eric," laughed Dawkins.

Maya was getting cramp in her legs from crouching. She slowly shifted position, trying to get the blood circulating again.

In the garage, Danny said: "I don't understand. Why don't you want Tony around?"

"Because he can't be trusted," said Eric menacingly.

"Can't be trusted with what?" Danny asked, sounding puzzled. "What are you planning, Mr Dawkins?"

"Now Danny," said Jack quietly. "Maybe it's better if you don't –"

Clunk!

Maya froze. Moving her leg to get comfortable, she'd accidentally kicked an empty oil can that must have been lying near her feet. It rattled loudly as it rolled away into the darkness.

"What was that?" yelled Eric, striding towards the door. "I hope no-one followed you here, Jack."

Chapter 6

Secrets, Secrets

Once Winnie had disappeared into the house, Joe hurdled the low fence at the back of the property, sneaked through the garden and up the side alley. As he was passing a window, a gas lamp suddenly flared to life, illuminating the passageway – and Joe. He quickly ducked back into the shadows.

When he'd got his heart back under control, he peeped over the windowsill. Through the half-open window he saw Winnie in her kitchen. She was opening a tin of cat food with a dangerous-looking claw-shaped knife, while a black cat nuzzled affectionately against her legs.

"Ha ha, Luci," she tittered. "Hungry, aren't you, my dear!" Then she sighed. "Now I've dug the hole, all I must do is find a child. A nice, strong boy would be best…."

Hearing this, Joe suddenly felt sick. He watched her spoon the blood-red chunks of fish into a bowl and place it on the floor.

"Here you are, Luci. Eat up!" The cat fell ravenously on the food. "Tomorrow is no good," Winnie said to herself. "That Morrison woman or one of her friends might come snooping around. No, I must do it on Saturday. Saturday is the best day, wouldn't you agree, Luci?" Lost in her thoughts, she picked up a carving knife that had been lying on the kitchen table and ran a finger gently along its blade. "Yes… Saturday…."

Then she yawned. "Goodnight, Luci. Sweet dreams." The light went out, leaving Joe in absolute darkness.

* * *

Maya ran for her life across the clearing and dived into the woods beyond, just as three figures came rushing out of the garage. "Over there!" she heard Eric shout. "Heading into those trees."

Heavy footsteps closed in on Maya as she dashed blindly through the wood. She stumbled over a tree root hidden in the undergrowth and fell headlong down a muddy bank. Hastily, she crawled beneath a natural ledge of earth and roots and curled up tight, breath surging from her lungs in ragged bursts.

A torch beam shone into her little hiding place, dazzling her. Maya put up a hand to shield her eyes.

"Well, well, if it ain't Maid Marion!" whispered Danny incredulously. "What are you doing here, and where's Robin?"

Maya stared up at his grinning face and was shocked at how oblivious he seemed to the danger both of them were in. She reached up and grabbed his wrist, pulling him under the ledge. He dropped the torch and the light went out.

"Hey, steady on!" he hissed.

"Don't trust those men, Danny!" she whispered urgently. "They're crooks. Both of them. Listen, promise me you won't go to that warehouse with Dawkins on Saturday. Do you promise?"

The boy stuttered, "I… I don't know…."

"Danny!" came Dawkins' voice from somewhere above them. "Where are you, lad?"

Danny looked at her for a moment, his smile fading. Then he crawled out into the open.

"What were you doing down there, son?" asked Jack.

"Tripped and fell," said Danny, retrieving his torch and climbing back up the bank.

"Did you catch sight of our little spy?" asked Eric.

"No, sir. Not a trace."

* * *

When a drenched and muddy Maya finally got back to their camp, she found Joe already there. The rain had stopped, fortunately, and Joe was trying and failing to get a fire started with a pile of damp twigs. Like her, he was shivering with cold as well as excitement. It took him half an hour, but Joe finally got the fire going. As its flames gradually put warmth back into their bones, they argued about where the danger lay for Danny.

"It has to be Winnie," insisted Joe. "I'm sure she wants to sacrifice Danny in a kind of ritual or something."

"But how's she ever going to get her hands on him if he's going to be over near Beaminster helping Dawkins and Swinburn steal stuff from a warehouse," said Maya.

"Maybe he never even got to the warehouse," suggested Joe. "Mrs Morrison said she saw him running across Vipers' Fold, remember?"

"Can you really see old Winnie the Witch chasing Danny across a meadow?" sighed Maya. "She must be sixty at least."

And so the arguments continued....

Traces of rosy light were already spreading through a grey eastern sky by the time they fell asleep.

Maya awoke at around 11 o'clock to sounds of birdsong and the sight of another plate of bread and cold beans sitting on the ground in front of her.

"Breakfast," smiled Joe.

As they ate, Joe made a suggestion: "We may not know who's responsible for Danny's disappearance, but we do know that it's going to happen tomorrow, Saturday the 19th. So why don't we timejump there right now."

"Okay," mumbled Maya through a mouthful of beans. "Let's do that – straight after breakfast."

* * *

The trees briefly faded, then came back into focus. Maya looked around. Saturday the 19th looked and felt no different to Friday the 18th – except maybe for a slight prickling of the neck hairs. Was it a little colder today – or was it the thought that this was the day Danny Doyle was due to disappear?

"What's the time?" Maya asked.

"Quarter to three," gasped Joe. "Sorry – that hasn't left us much time. I can choose the date with this phone, but I haven't yet figured out how to choose the time!"

"We have to get going," said Maya, already marching off down the path. "I just hope we're not too late. No way can we let Danny go to that warehouse.

* * *

Twenty minutes later, they were on Charlton Abbas High Street. "Where do you reckon Michael and Danny's house is?" Maya asked.

"They said they were staying with the Welbridges," said Joe. "Mr Watkins in the village shop will be able to tell us where they live."

They were about to head over there when they saw Michael or Danny coming towards them. As he got closer, Maya guessed which twin it was from the worried frown he was wearing.

"Hey, Michael," she called. "Have you seen your brother around?"

He looked up, and his face brightened. "There you are!" he said. "I was looking for you two all day yesterday. Where have you been?"

"Never mind that. Have you seen Danny?" Joe asked urgently.

Michael shook his head. "He may be at home. We can go there now, if you like."

"Come on then, quickly," Joe replied.

As they followed him, Joe nudged Maya. "Remember what old man Michael said? He said he saw Danny for the last time this afternoon, and Danny told him he was on his way to the warehouse. That meeting hasn't happened yet, so that's good news."

Michael led them to a cottage with a slate roof and white, wisteria-clad walls. He knocked on the door, and a kindly looking grey-haired lady opened it.

"Auntie Vi," said Michael. "These are my friends, Joe and Maya."

Auntie Vi gazed smilingly at them over the top of her half-moon spectacles. "Friends! How nice! Won't you come in?"

She held the door wide and they trooped into the cottage's front room, brushing the twigs and bits of leaves from their coats. It was small and homely, with well-padded armchairs, framed pictures on the mantelpiece, a gas fire and a large wooden radio in the corner. On the sofa sat a middle-aged man and woman sipping tea. Maya thought she'd seen the woman somewhere before, though she couldn't think where.

"Afternoon, Michael," the couple on the sofa chorused.

"Afternoon Mr and Mrs Abbott," answered Michael. Then he turned to Auntie Vi. "Is Danny home, Auntie?"

"Danny? I haven't seen him since this morning. But you know how hard it is to keep track of that boy.

Always flying off somewhere or other." She suddenly went pale. "You don't suppose he's gone off with that dreadful Dawkins fellow do you?"

"Calm yourself Violet, dear," said Mrs Abbott. "Daniel is a very sensible lad. Just like Michael, here. He wouldn't do anything stupid." She sighed. "We do so miss having young people about the house, since our… you know."

"Of course, dear," said Auntie Vi, sympathetically. "And if you ever need any help from one of my boys, any time at all, you only need ask."

Joe nudged Maya and pointed to his watch. It was nearly half past three.

"Can I get you a glass of milk, children?" Auntie Vi asked. "Or some cake. It's got cocoa powder in it. And real eggs. None of that powdered muck around here. We keep our own chick–"

"Sorry," said Maya, as she and Joe edged towards the front door. "That's really kind of you, but we've got to, like, be heading off now."

Michael looked disappointed. "Did you want me to come with–?"

"Of course!" smiled Maya.

Once they were on the street, Joe asked Michael: "Where were you heading just now, when we stopped you on the high street?"

Michael looked confused. "Why do you want to know?"

"It's really important," said Joe. He glanced at Maya, then took a deep breath. "Look, Michael. Danny is going to disappear this afternoon, but before he does, he's going to meet you, and he's going to tell you that he's on the way to a warehouse near Beaminster. If you can take us to where you were about to go, hopefully we'll find him there, and we may be able to stop him disappearing…."

Michael was staring at him. "H-how can you know all this?"

Joe sighed. He seemed unsure how to go on.

"Michael, listen up," Maya broke in. "It's like this, we're from the future."

"That's right," continued Joe. "And unless we can stop what's about to happen, you're going to spend the rest of your life looking for Danny. Now please tell us where you were going."

"You're from the future! *My* future?" said Michael, backing away from them, a scared smile dawning on his face. "This is a joke, right? You're pulling my leg." He glanced around. "Did Kellaway put you up to this?"

Maya took his hand and gazed deeply into his nervous, blinking eyes. "We want to save Danny," she said. "Please help us. Where were you going just now?"

"I was… going to the wreck."

"The wreck?"

"Yeah, an RAF Hurricane crashed in a field near here last summer. Sometimes I like to… spend time there, you know, looking for shrapnel and stuff."

"Well, let's go there now!" said Maya, prodding Michael forwards. He led them back to the high street, where he turned left.

Michael seemed in a semi-daze. "Danny's really going to disappear today," he murmured, shaking his head. "I can't believe it. Do you think that Dawkins…?"

"We don't know," answered Joe. "Mrs Morrison will be the last person to see your brother. She'll see him running through Vipers' Fold this evening, so maybe nothing will happen at the warehouse."

Michael stared at Joe wonderingly. He seemed about to say something when a dark green Morris van went roaring past them.

Maya spun around just in time to see Dawkins in the driving seat, with Danny next to him.

"That was them!" she cried. "We're too late."

They watched despairingly as the van hurtled along the high street. Then it suddenly screeched to a halt outside the village shop. Dawkins and Danny got out and walked into the shop.

Maya was already sprinting towards them.

"Hang on!" cried Joe, catching up with her and pulling her around to face him. "What are you planning to do?"

"I'm going to make sure Danny doesn't go to that warehouse, of course," she said.

"What if he won't listen?" said Joe. "Look. I've got a better plan."

Chapter 7

The Stowaways

Joe raced to the van and pulled open the back doors.

"There's an old blanket in here we can hide under," he shouted. "They won't see us. Quick! Get in!"

Maya stared at him, surprised. It wasn't like Joe to be this daring. But he was right: they had more chance of rescuing Danny this way.

"Okay!" she said, climbing after Joe into the back of the van.

Michael hesitated.

"Come on!" hissed Maya.

He got in just as Danny and Dawkins emerged from the shop, and Maya quickly shut the doors. The three stowaways hastily crawled under the grubby blanket. There was no partition between the front seats and the rear of the van, so they had to lie completely quiet and still. Michael uttered a small whimper of fear, until Maya covered his mouth with her hand.

The van rocked slightly as Danny and Dawkins jumped in. Then the front doors slammed shut and, with a cough and splutter, the engine started. Beneath the musty old blanket smell, Maya caught a whiff of Dawkins' cheap aftershave.

She poked her head out for some air and was immediately hit in the face by a bouquet of flowers, lobbed into the back by Dawkins.

"Eric's wife'll love those, Danny boy," Dawkins chuckled. "Flowers – quickest way to a woman's heart, let me tell you! Have to keep her sweet, see, 'cause we may need another favour from her in future!" He made a grinding gear change as they picked up speed. "I just hope she's put enough 'you know what' in Tony's sandwich!"

"What has she put in his sandwich, Mr Dawkins?" Danny asked.

"Never you mind," Dawkins chuckled.

Dawkins was a poor driver, taking the bends way too fast. Maya, Joe and Michael were jolted about and frequently slammed painfully against the van's bare metal walls. At one point Dawkins seemed to get lost. They heard him curse. "Now they've gone and painted over all the road signs. Never mind fooling the blinking Nazis, what about us poor Brits?"

Eventually, the journey ended in a screeching halt. The children heard the scrape of a large door being opened, and the van rolled forward into a giant, gloomy space. Peering through the grimy back window, they glimpsed racks of boxes piled up on shelves reaching up to the roof – this had to be the warehouse.

As the back doors opened they buried themselves

deeper under the blanket, rigid with fear. A long silence followed. Had they been spotted? Was the blanket about to be ripped away?

There was a sudden jolting bang beside them. A heavy box had been tossed into the van, landing just inches from Maya's knee. Another box quickly followed. And another. Michael squealed as it bashed against his ribs, but luckily no one heard.

Then, from a distance, they heard a voice – a surprised voice.

"Hey, you! What's going on here?"

There was a grunt of surprise. "Tony?" came an answering voice that Maya recognized as Eric's. "What are you doing back here? You were supposed to be… I mean I thought you were sick."

"I was, but now I'm feeling better. What are these people doing here, Eric?"

"Now listen Tony, I –"

Whump!

They heard a strangled groan and a thud as if something heavy had fallen to the floor.

"Blimey, Jack! You've – you've knocked him out!" cried Eric. "Now we're in real trouble."

"You mean *you're* in trouble, Eric," replied Dawkins coldly. "This part of it was down to you. You were supposed to guarantee we wouldn't be disturbed. Now it's up to you to sort out the mess. Come on, Danny. We've got enough stuff. Let's get out of here… Danny? Hey, son, what's wrong?"

"It's all wrong, Mr Dawkins," came Danny's worried,

disappointed voice. "You told me you were legit… a 'businessman'. You lied to me."

"Come on now, son. Get in the van. We can talk about it later."

The two of them got back in. There was a hasty u-turn, a squeal of tyres and, once again, they were speeding along the road. As they drove, Dawkins kept up a constant smooth patter, using all his charm to try to win Danny around, but the boy said very little in reply.

They turned right on to the bumpy, twisty track that led to Dawkins' secret lock-up in the woods.

Suddenly the van swerved, violently.

"Hey Danny!' cried the alarmed Dawkins. 'What are you doing? Get off!"

The van lurched one way, then the other.

Risking a peek above the blanket, Maya saw that Danny was leaning over to the driver's side, one hand gripping the steering wheel. He was pulling and pushing it, making the van veer wildly from right to left.

"You gone mad, boy?" cried the now scared Dawkins. "You're gonna kill us both!"

Abruptly, Danny let go of the steering wheel, opened the passenger door and jumped out of the still-moving van. Dawkins slammed on the brakes, causing the three in the back to fly forwards. Maya hit her head on the back of the front seat. Through a dazed blur, she glimpsed Dawkins reaching under his seat and pulling out something that gleamed – a gun! Then he leapt out of the van and tore into the forest after Danny.

"Quick!" cried Joe. "We have to get to Danny before Dawkins does!"

They fell out of the van and plunged into the wood.

"Which way did they go?" queried Maya.

"That way," said Michael, pointing to a clearing through the trees. "Right by your camp."

"Dawkins has got a gun," Maya told the others as they ran towards the clearing.

"A gun!" squeaked Michael in a terrified voice.

"Well then we need to arm ourselves," Joe murmured. He retrieved his bow and arrow from where he'd hidden it inside their makeshift shelter, and handed Maya his penknife.

"What about me?" gulped Michael.

"You just stick close to us," Maya reassured him.

Joe glanced at his watch. "It's quarter past six. Danny will be in Vipers' Fold in fifteen minutes, so let's get over there."

Michael led them on a short cut through the trees. As Winnie's cottage loomed ahead of them, Maya noticed Joe stiffen.

"The old witch said she was going to make her sacrifice today," he whispered. He glanced towards Michael, checking he was out of earshot. "I just hope Danny hasn't ended up as her victim."

They slowly rounded the cottage, keeping well within the trees, in case Winnie happened to be looking out of a window. From the back garden they heard a grunting, panting sound, as if someone was struggling with something. Joe went very pale.

"What's going on?" whined Michael.

Maya ran to the fence to get a closer look. She peered over, and could hardly believe her eyes.

Simon Kellaway, of all people, was in Winnie's garden, slowly dragging the dead body of a pig towards the hole that Winnie had dug in her vegetable patch. Winnie was walking alongside him, thanking him profusely.

Maya beckoned to the boys, and they came and joined her at the fence.

"So lucky you were passing, lad," Winnie was saying to Simon, "The food inspectors'll be coming on Monday, and if they see this pig, they're bound to reduce my rations. That's why I had to kill it and hide it."

"Yes, Mrs Coombes," grunted Simon.

"But there was no way I could drag it all the way out here meself," she went on. And I couldn't ask a grown-up to help me, because they all hate me. They'd find any excuse to shop me to the authorities. But you can trust a child. I can trust you, can't I, Simon?"

"So long as you give me that half crown and pound of sausages you promised me, you old witch," muttered Kellaway, half under his breath.

Maya saw the smile of relief slowly breaking across Joe's face. So Winnie hadn't been planning to sacrifice a child after all – she'd only wanted to hide an illicit pig!

Maya smiled, too, until her attention was caught by a darting movement to her left. She turned in time to see, beyond Winnie's back fence, a small figure sprinting through the long grass of Vipers' Fold.

Danny!

And running hard, just ten metres behind him, gun in hand, was Jack Dawkins.

"Joe, look!" Maya gasped, before dashing alongside the fence towards the meadow.

Joe and Michael soon joined her there. "There's Mrs Morrison," panted Michael, pointing through the trees behind them. "She'll stop Dawkins."

Maya turned and saw the postmistress, just visible on the forest path. Mrs Morrison was staring at Danny as he raced through the grass. But she obviously couldn't see Dawkins tearing after him. She just shook her head, got back on her bike and cycled away.

The time, according to Joe's watch, was 6.30.

"Just like you said it would happen!" cried Michael.

Danny was going like the wind, but Dawkins was gaining on him.

"Come on!" cried Maya, starting to run into the meadow. Then she faltered. Dawkins had caught up with the boy. He had him by the collar. The spiv had lost his pork pie hat and his smart jacket. His face was purple from rage and exhaustion. He was shaking Danny, pointing his gun at him and yelling, though they couldn't hear what he was saying.

"He's going to kill him," cried Maya. "We have to do something!" But she sensed they were too late. By the time they reached them, Danny would probably be dead.

Joe, however, had other plans. She saw him going down on one knee. He drew back the string of his bow and squinted down the shaft of the arrow he'd placed there.

With a dull twang and a whisper on the air, the arrow took flight. It arced through the sky on a direct line towards Dawkins. Maya didn't see it land, but she saw Dawkins jerk, give a yell of pain and look down in shock at his leg.

Danny took his opportunity and charged away in the direction of the village. Dawkins started limping after him, then raised his gun as if to shoot the boy. As he did so, another arrow flew out of Joe's bow. Dawkins cried out and grasped his hand. His gun went flying into the grass. Joe stared, hardly daring to believe what he'd just done, as Dawkins howled with rage, pain and frustration.

"Brilliant shooting, Joe," laughed Maya, slapping him on the back.

Michael let out a whoop of joy. "You've saved Danny!" he cried.

His brother was now a speck in the distance, close to the outskirts of the village. But the danger wasn't quite over.

They saw Dawkins stoop to retrieve his gun and begin limping furiously towards them. It was time to make their own escape.

Chapter 8

Gone!

The three caught up with Danny on Charlton Abbas High Street.

"Robin Hood and Maid Marion!" he grinned when he saw them. His face glowed in the dying light of the day. "Your timing, as ever, was perfect!"

"We're just glad you're safe," smiled Maya.

"I should have listened to you, Mikey," Danny said to his brother. "You were right when you told me not to trust that man."

"Speaking of Dawkins, he's still after you," Joe reminded Danny. "You'd better get home now and tell Auntie Vi all about it. She can explain to the police how you were innocent in all this."

"The police!" gasped Danny. "I didn't think they'd be involved."

Just then, a car coasted to a stop near where they were standing. It was sleek and shiny black with beautiful curves and a soft top.

"Evening, Mr and Mrs Abbott," smiled Danny

cheekily. "Taking the Jag out for a little spin are we?"

Maya recognized the middle-aged couple from earlier that day. Once again, she was struck by the thought that she'd seen Mrs Abbott somewhere before.

The Abbotts were pale with worry. "We've been out looking for you, Danny," said Mrs Abbott. "There was a report on the wireless just now about a break-in at a warehouse. The police are searching for that rogue Jack Dawkins. You weren't involved by any chance, were you?"

Danny nodded, a bit shamefaced. "I'm afraid I was, Mrs Abbott. You aren't going to turn me in though, are you?"

Mrs Abbott smiled and shook her head. "Of course not, dear, but…." She beckoned him closer to the window. "We can hide you for a bit until all the fuss dies down. We've talked to Violet about it and she agrees it's for the best."

Mr Abbott leaned across his wife and winked at Danny: "We've all done things we regret, young man. That's what growing up's all about. Now hop in, and we'll take you somewhere safe."

Maya, Joe and Michael watched Danny step gleefully into the back seat of the beautiful car. Danny grinned and waved at them as Mr Abbott drove away.

Maya felt a vague sense of unease as she watched them go, but she suppressed it and waved back.

Everything was fine now. Wasn't it?

* * *

When they got back to Auntie Vi's house, they were in for a shock.

"The Abbotts said what?" she spluttered. "I never agreed to any such thing!" She began putting on her hat and coat. "I'm going straight over to their house this minute. They've no right to take Danny anywhere without asking me first."

As she opened the door to leave, Mrs Morrison came bustling in, full of news that she simply had to impart. "Oh, hello there, Violet, dear. You know, I just saw your young Danny running through Vipers' Fold. Some children's game, I expect. But, listen, what I really came to tell you about was the Abbotts."

"Don't talk to me about the Abbotts," grimaced Auntie Vi, pushing her way past her.

"So you know they've left then?" said Mrs Morrison.

"Left?" Auntie Vi stopped in her tracks.

"Yes, gone. Without so much as a goodbye."

"Do you know where they were going?" asked Joe.

"I know where they came from," answered Mrs Morrison, "because they had their letters forwarded to my post office when they first moved here. Tyler Terrace, I think it was. Slade Common. Yes, that was it."

Maya gave a start when she heard this. Slade Common was where she lived in London. Now she remembered where she'd seen Mrs Abbott before. It was in a photograph her historian father was planning to use in his *History of Slade Common*. Something had happened to the Abbotts. He'd told her about it once. Now what was it? If only she'd paid more attention.

"Mrs Welbridge," Maya said to Auntie Vi, "Can you take us to the nearest train station? We have to get to Slade Common!"

Auntie Vi, Joe, Michael and Mrs Morrison all stared at her.

"Well, I really think we ought to go to the police, dear," said Auntie Vi. "In fact, I think I'll go straight round to Mr Kellaway now."

"You don't need to do that," Maya reassured her. "I know where Danny is, and I can get him back for you."

The urgency in Maya's voice seemed to impress Auntie Vi. She sensed she was telling the truth "Very well," she said. "But you can't go now. The last train left Dorchester half an hour ago, and what with the bombing and all…. Why don't you stay with us for the night? You can catch the first train tomorrow morning."

Mrs Morrison spoke to Mr Watkins, who agreed to drive Maya and Joe to Dorchester station in his delivery van. Auntie Vi put Maya in Danny's bed and Joe was given a spare mattress.

As they lay in bed, unable to sleep, Maya explained to Joe about the photo of Mrs Abbott that her dad had shown her. "I think there was some awful story attached to that photo, Joe," she whispered. "I just can't remember what it was – and now I'm really worried for Danny."

* * *

The next morning, after breakfast, Auntie Vi and Michael gave them each a hug before they set off. They both had tears in their eyes.

"Bring him back safely" Michael whispered to Maya.

"We will," she promised.

They were at Dorchester station ticket office, and Mr Watkins' van had disappeared back to Charlton Abbas, before they realized they didn't have enough money to pay the fare to Waterloo,

"We'll just have to get platform tickets, and hope for the best," said Maya.

They waited nervously for the train to arrive. Eventually it came chugging in, pistons pumping, engine whistling, shrouded in steam like some mysterious iron monster.

"A real steam train!" cried Joe.

They clambered aboard and Joe leaned out of the window as the train began picking up speed. There was a loud whistle as they entered a tunnel, and Joe got a faceful of smoke. Maya laughed at his grinning, soot-covered face.

The journey took forever, and the train seemed to stop at every station. At Clapham Junction a crowd of noisy schoolchildren got on.

"I can't believe they're on a school trip in the middle of the Blitz," whispered Joe.

"I can't believe we made it all the way up here on a penny platform ticket," grinned Maya.

As they reached central London, Joe and Maya were shocked into silence by the sight of so many bombed-out buildings, fires still smouldering among the ruins. Scrawny children dressed in rags played on the rubble. Now, more than ever, Maya began to realize what danger Danny might be in.

At 11.30, the train finally puffed into the giant shed of Waterloo Station. They got off, and looked anxiously towards the ticket inspector at the barrier.

"How are we going to get past her?" Joe asked despairingly. "If we're caught, we've had it."

Chapter 9

Tired and Hungry

As Maya and Joe wondered how to get past the ticket inspector, Maya caught sight of the group of schoolchildren they'd seen earlier. They were being shepherded towards the barrier by a harassed-looking teacher. This gave Maya an idea. "Why don't we pretend to be part of that group of kids," she suggested to Joe. "The ticket inspector might not notice us."

"But they look about nine, and they're all in uniform," Joe pointed out. "We'll stick out like a sore thumb."

"It's worth a try, isn't it?" said Maya, running to catch up with the school party. "Quick. Do your coat up. She might not notice."

"This is your craziest idea yet," whispered Joe as they joined the back of the group. "And that's saying something!"

"Come on, you wimp!" giggled Maya.

Crouching to make themselves appear smaller, Maya and Joe edged their way towards the middle of the group. They began attracting stares from some of the children. Maya hushed them with a fingertip to her lips. "We're working for the government… on a secret mission," she whispered. "Don't tell anyone."

The children stared at them with big, round eyes, but luckily said nothing.

Soon, they were through the barrier. They glanced back to see the ticket inspector frowning. The number of heads she'd counted through didn't tally with the number of tickets the teacher had handed her. Then the inspector looked up and saw Maya and Joe. Her face turned red with fury.

"Run!" cried Maya.

They didn't stop until they were safely on the street outside the station.

"How are we going to get to Slade Common without any money?" Joe asked, once he'd caught his breath.

"We'll have to walk," said Maya.

"How far is it?"

"Not sure. About seven miles I think."

Joe shrugged. "Better get going then."

It was hard to make progress at first. Central London was a mess. After eight months of bombing, the streets were full of holes and strewn with debris. Many of the buildings were shattered, windowless shells. Chunks of concrete and bricks and collapsed girders spilled outwards from the ruins on to the pavements. It was as if a giant with heavy boots had stomped all over the city. But what struck Maya most was the attitude of the people they passed. They saw businessmen in their suits going to work, mothers pushing prams, shopkeepers offering their wares from their semi-ruined premises. Buses, cars and bikes wove their way through the rubble. The city was moving. People looked a bit shabby and worn out, but they were stubbornly carrying on with their lives.

Maya and Joe gradually made their way down the Old Kent Road, through Peckham, New Cross and Deptford. In Lewisham High Street, they saw a crowd of destitute people queuing for a bowl of soup from a mobile kitchen. Hungry and now penniless, Maya and Joe joined the line. The soup was tepid and watery, but better than nothing.

They reached Slade Common at just before three o'clock.

Mrs Morrison had said that the Abbotts had lived on Tyler Terrace, so the chances were that this was where they'd gone. The street lay opposite the common and round the corner from Mycroft Place, Maya's home.

As they drew closer, she scented something charred in the breeze. It gave her a sense of foreboding.

Maya's first impression, as they turned the corner, was that the street of neat terraced houses was not so different from the one she remembered.

Except for one of the houses.

The third house on the right had been almost completely destroyed. All that remained was a flame-blackened carcass of exposed timbers and interior rooms. The front wall had collapsed and had slid all over the street. A Jaguar car, parked by the kerb, lay crushed beneath the debris. The upper floors of the house had sagged, and a sofa and a piano sat incongruously on top of the piles of brick and plaster on the pavement. The houses to either side were remarkably untouched, apart from a blackening of their paintwork and roof tiles.

Maya raised her hands to her mouth as a sickly feeling spread through her insides. The sight brought it all back to her. Now she remembered exactly what her dad had told her that day when he showed her the photo of Mrs Abbott. The Abbotts' house had been destroyed in a bomb attack in April 1941, near the end of the Blitz – the only direct hit Slade Common received during the war.

If only she had remembered this yesterday!

"That's their house," she said in a cracked voice.

"Do you think they…?" Joe couldn't complete the sentence.

Maya shook her head sadly. "No one survived."

"So that was how Danny disappeared," said Joe.

"It happened last night," said a soft voice behind them. They turned to see an elderly man staring at the ruin. "I live round the corner," he said. "Saw them arriving late last night. A charming couple. They'd been away for a year or so, living in some village in Dorset."

"We knew them," said Maya, weakly.

"Then you'll know they had a boy with them – poor child. None of them stood a chance… Ironic, wouldn't you say? They must have left London to get away from the bombs, and the minute they come back…."

"What time did the bomb fall last night?" Joe asked him.

"Just after midnight."

"Thank you, Mr... Mr...."

"Davenport," said the man, tipping his hat and turning to leave. "It was nice meeting you. I'm so sorry about your friends."

Maya saw Joe's hand reaching for his pocket, and she immediately knew what he was thinking.

Joe shifted the dials on the timephone to the previous night.

"We can't stop this from happening," he said through gritted teeth. "But we can at least try to save Danny... and the Abbotts."

Maya nodded and held tight to his arm.

The world faded first to grey, and then to darkness.

Joe looked at his watch. "Ten past eleven. We've got fifty minutes before the bomb falls."

Fog drifted in waves down Tyler Terrace, making the street look ghostly and abandoned. The third house on the right now looked just like all the others. At the edges of the blackout blind in its front room window, they glimpsed a light burning. The Abbotts' Jaguar was parked outside.

They were in there right now! Maya wondered how Danny was feeling. He was probably scared and disoriented.

She and Joe walked up to the door and knocked.

After a moment, the door opened. Mr Abbott stood there in his pyjamas.

"Hello?" he enquired. And then, like an electric shock, a ripple of fear passed across his face. It was quickly replaced by an amiable smile. "Well, if it isn't Danny's friends from Charlton Abbas. This is a surprise! What are you two doing here?"

Maya decided to come straight to the point. "Mr Abbott, your house is going to be hit by a bomb in less than one hour. You, your wife and Danny must leave here immediately."

Mr Abbott uttered a nervous laugh. "Is this some sort of joke?"

"Who is it, John?" came a voice from within the house.

"It's Danny's friends," said Mr Abbott. "You know, dear, the ones he was telling us about on the journey. Joe and Maya. They say there's going to be a bomb and we have to leave the house." He twinkled at them as he said this, as if it was all an amusing prank and he wanted to be in on it. "Look, why don't you both come in? You must be tired."

Maya exchanged glances with Joe. "We'll come in for a minute, Mr Abbott," she said. "But we're serious about this bomb."

"Yes, of course you are," chuckled Mr Abbott, standing aside to let them enter. "But tell me, how on earth did you find us?"

Before they could think of what to say to this, Mrs Abbott appeared in the hallway. She stared at them as if at a pair of ghosts, twisting the hem of her nightdress in her hands.

"Where's Danny?" Maya asked.

"Asleep," smiled Mr Abbott. "The poor boy was exhausted after his ordeal this afternoon, and then the journey. Here, let me take your coats."

"We really haven't got time for this, Mr Abbott," protested Maya.

"Of course you have," he said affably, as he helped them out of their coats and placed them on a set of pegs next to an old grandfather clock.

"John, I need to talk to you," said Mrs Abbott, her eyes never leaving Maya and Joe. She pulled him towards the front room.

"Be with you in a mo," Mr Abbott called cheerfully before the door closed behind them.

Joe and Maya, now alone in the corridor, stared at each other.

"How are we going to get them to believe us?" asked Joe.

"We should go and fetch Danny right now," ventured Maya, making for the staircase. "If we can get him out of here, the Abbotts are bound to follow."

Before she could reach the first step, Mr Abbott suddenly reappeared and blocked her way.

"If you're looking for Danny, you won't find him up there," he said. "He's in our… downstairs bedroom. As I said, Danny's asleep at the moment, but if you really want to see him…." He gestured towards a door beneath the staircase. "Be our guest."

Maya and Joe moved towards the door. Maya opened it and they peered into the darkness beyond.

"Go on," urged Mr Abbott. "Don't you want to say hello to your friend?"

She felt a sudden, violent shove from behind, and the two of them toppled forwards through the doorway.

The door slammed closed behind them, plunging them into darkness. There was a metallic click of a key being turned in a lock.

Chapter 10

Prisoners!

"Let us out!" screamed Maya, banging on the door.

There was no reply.

Maya sighed. "How could we have been so stupid?"

Joe uttered a groan of pain.

"You okay, Joe?" she asked.

"I–I think so," he said. "Bumped my head."

They groped their way down a set of steep, narrow steps. It felt cold and there was a strong smell of damp – nothing like a bedroom. After a brief fumble, Maya located a light switch.

A bare, low-wattage lightbulb hanging from the ceiling illuminated a small, brick-lined cellar. The room was full of old-looking objects, all of them covered in a thick layer of dust and cobwebs. There was a cot and a Victorian-style pram, a set of wooden skittles, a rocking-horse, a child's handcart filled with wooden blocks, and stacks of puzzles, games and books. On a shelf lay an ancient-looking cricket bat. A small, white linen surplice, as worn by an altar boy, hung from a coatstand.

"We have to get out of here," said Maya. "Can you use the timephone to go back a few minutes – to just before the door was locked?"

Joe reached into his pocket. "It's hard to be that exact with time travel, but –" He stopped and went very pale.

"What is it?"

Joe was desperately patting his pockets. "The timephone – I don't have it! Must have left it in the pocket of my coat upstairs."

They gaped at each other.

"We're stuck then," said Joe bleakly. He checked his watch. "We've got twenty-eight minutes to find a way out of here."

Maya looked around the bare, windowless walls, searching for an opening. They spent the next ten minutes making a methodical search of the room, pushing aside toys, chests and bookcases for an exit – but could find no way out.

Maya ran up the stairs and began banging on the door.

"Let us out!" she yelled again and again.

After several minutes of this, they heard Mrs Abbott's severe yet fragile voice.

"We know why you're here," she said. "You've come to take Danny away from us…. Well, we won't let you. We've lost one son. We're not going to lose another!"

"You can have Danny," cried Maya desperately. "We're just trying to save your lives…" she gave a small sob, "… and ours."

They heard receding footsteps heading back up the hallway.

Maya had never felt so scared or helpless.

She felt Joe's arm around her shoulder and she squeezed him back.

Time slipped by. She could hear the ticking of the grandfather clock in the hall. "Five minutes," she whispered.

From where they were sitting, at the top of the staircase, they had a clear view across the top of the cellar. Maya noticed a shadowy recess in one corner of the ceiling. It was covered in cobwebs, so hadn't been visible from the cellar floor. The wall beneath was stained black. Was it a coal chute?

Peering closer at the recess, she saw it had a rectangular iron plate set within it, and her heart beat faster. That could lead them out on to the pavement!

She nudged Joe and pointed to it.

They ran down the stairs and, together, dragged the rocking-horse across the floor so that it was positioned beneath the iron plate. Joe grabbed the cricket bat, then climbed on to the saddle of the wooden horse. Maya crossed her fingers so tightly they hurt, as Joe, wobbling precariously, reached up through the cobwebs with the cricket bat and tried to push open the plate. There was a metallic clunk, but the plate didn't shift. He tried again, harder.

The plate was stuck fast.

Joe slumped back to the floor, defeated.

From upstairs, they heard the chime of the grandfather clock.

"Oh, no," said Maya softly. "It's twelve o'clock."

Joe charged back up the stairs and began banging on it furiously.

The fourth chime sounded.

"Save yourselves!" he yelled. "Get out of the house!"

The bell chimed a fifth time.

Suddenly, there was a click and the door opened.

Danny stood there, looking sleepy and surprised.

He was knocked backwards, as Joe and Maya flew out into the hallway. "Quick!" cried Maya, grabbing Danny's hand. "We have to get out right now!"

Mr and Mrs Abbott were standing in front of the door, blocking their way.

Mrs Abbott was crying. "Don't take our boy from us!" she wailed.

The eighth chime sounded.

From far above came the faint drone of an aircraft.

"Hear that?" cried Joe. "That plane is carrying your bomb."

Mr Abbott stared at him intensely, then turned to his wife.

"Rose. You don't think…?"

The twelfth and final chime sounded. The noise of the bomber got louder and louder.

Maya, still clutching Danny's hand, charged forwards. Joe grabbed his coat from the peg and followed in her wake. She pushed aside Mr Abbott, pulled open the front door and the three of them ran out into the night. The drone of the aircraft was fading. In the ensuing silence Maya heard the faint whistle of an object falling rapidly through the air.

Mr Abbott must have heard it, too, or else he had a change of heart, because he suddenly grabbed his wife's arm and dragged her out of the house.

As he did so, Maya glanced up and saw something big and dark crash through the roof.

"Run!" she screamed, and she began sprinting up the street.

BOOM!!!

It was by far the loudest, most violent thing she'd ever experienced – beyond sound, it was like a physical force that ripped the ground from beneath her. It was a scorching blast at her back that lifted her up and flung her headlong through the air. She landed in a bruising tumble in the middle of the road.

There were muffled screams and crashes behind her. She felt numb.

Then a hand reached down and helped her to her feet. It was Danny, bruised and soot-smeared. "Perfect timing – again!" he grinned.

Maya was filled with relief to see Joe limping up to join them. She gave him a hug. "That was close," she sniffed.

"Too close," whispered Joe.

A few metres away, Mr and Mrs Abbott were sitting amid the rubble, staring at the ruin of their home. The burning embers reflected in their smudged, tear-stained cheeks. They looked dazed, but unhurt.

"Thank you," Danny said to Maya and Joe. "But how did you know?"

"We're – we're from the future," said Joe.

Danny stared at him as if he was mad. "What do you mean?"

"We're from the twenty-first century, and we travelled back in time to change the past."

"In the original version of history, you died in this bomb," Maya told Danny. "Your brother never knew what happened, and he spent his whole life searching for you."

Danny shivered. "What you're saying sounds… mad. But it also kind of makes sense of everything that's happened. I mean, that's how you knew I was going to be in Vipers' Fold this afternoon, right?" He stared at the wreckage of the house. "So Mikey spent his life searching for me." His voice trailed away as he blinked back some tears. "Well, he doesn't need to worry now. He can come and join us."

"But what about your own parents, Danny?" Maya asked. "Won't they want you back?"

"I doubt it," Danny replied. "They didn't want us much when we were living at home, and they haven't written to us the whole time we've been in Dorset. They might be dead for all we know."

Danny switched his gaze to the Abbotts. "They're nice people – I mean it. Just heartbroken after losing their son – and really scared you were trying to take me away from them."

Mrs Abbott turned around to face Maya and Joe. "We're so sorry," she wept. "You were very courageous. I wish we'd believed you. Our beloved son George… he died last year on the 18th of August. A German plane…

crashed into that church over there." She pointed at the church across the common. "He was the only one in there at the time…. He was an altar boy. Danny reminded us so much of our George. I know we were wrong to take him, but losing our son left such a hole in our lives…."

"You left a hole in Michael's life," said Maya.

"We never wanted that," said Mr Abbott. "We were planning to sort things out with Violet, invite Michael to come and live with us, too." Then he returned his bleak gaze to the ruins. "Though I'm not sure exactly where we'll be living now. We may have to go back to Dorset."

"You can come and stay with me for a bit, if you like," said a voice behind them. They turned to see Mr Davenport standing there.

"I live in Mycroft Place, round the corner," Davenport explained. "It's a big place for one man on his own. I'd be glad of the company. You can stay there for as long as you like, or until you get yourselves sorted out."

Mr and Mrs Abbott, and Danny, looked very grateful for the offer. As the four of them talked it over, Maya turned to Joe. "I think it's time we made tracks, wouldn't you say, cuz?"

Joe nodded. "We've done what we came for."

They crossed the road and walked on to the common. When they were sure they were out of sight of everyone, Maya took his hand, and Joe began twirling the dials on the timephone….

She thought of an old man, living alone in his house

in the woods, with a room full of letters and a sad, mysterious hole in his life. Then she thought of two happy boys, soon to be reunited in a beautiful house – *her house!* – and her heart filled with joy.

THE END

FICTI⬤N EXPRESS

THE READERS TAKE CONTROL!

Have you ever wanted to change the course of a plot, change a character's destiny, tell an author what to write next?

Well, now you can!

'The Disappearance of Danny Doyle' was originally written for the award-winning interactive e-book website Fiction Express.

Fiction Express e-books are published in gripping weekly episodes. At the end of each episode, readers are given voting options to decide where the plot goes next. They vote online and the winning vote is then conveyed to the author who writes the next episode, in real time, according to the readers' most popular choice.

www.fictionexpress.co.uk

WINNER
Education Resources
Award for Innovation

FICTION EXPRESS

TALK TO THE AUTHORS

The Fiction Express website features a blog where readers can interact with the authors while they are writing. An exciting and unique opportunity!

FANTASTIC TEACHER RESOURCES

Each weekly Fiction Express episode comes with a PDF of teacher resources packed with ideas to extend the text.

"The teaching resources are fab and easily fill a whole week of literacy lessons!"
Rachel Humphries, teacher at Westacre Middle School

Have you read the first Time Detectives book –
***The Mystery of Maddie Musgrove* – yet?**
Here is a taster for you…

Chapter 1

An Amazing Discovery

Joe stared up in horror. A plane was falling out of the sky, trailing clouds of black smoke. It was heading straight towards him! Terrified, he turned and began to run through the graveyard. He ran so fast he lost his balance and tumbled, scratching his bare knees and banging his head on a gravestone.

Glancing behind, he saw the dark shape of the plane closing in on him, engine screaming, fire spurting from its wings. He shut his eyes tight and waited. There was a massive roar and a ripping, smashing sound. Heat from the blast scorched his face. A horrible burning smell filled his nostrils, making him choke.

Slowly, Joe opened his eyes. The plane had crashed metres from where he lay. It must have blown up on impact because there was hardly anything left but a charred, smoking wreck. The gravestone had saved his life, shielding his body from the full force of the explosion. Only the plane's tail had survived intact. Joe's blood turned cold when he glimpsed the sign on the tail. It was a black cross – the symbol of the German Luftwaffe in the Second World War.

With a shaking hand, he reached through the long grass for the smartphone that had slipped from his grasp when he'd fallen. He prayed it wasn't broken.

The screen lit up. Thank goodness!

Nervously, he touched the "Timeshift" icon, scanned the screen and then touched "Emergency return".

* * *

The scene changed immediately. He was still lying there in the churchyard, but the wreck of the plane had disappeared. It was now a peaceful, sunny day. The only smell was fresh-mown grass, and the only sound was birdsong. Everything, in fact, was exactly as it ought to be.

A wave of relief washed through him. Had he dreamed the whole thing? It hadn't felt like a dream. And his face still felt tender from the burning heat.

"Joe! Where are you?"

He looked up to see his cousin Maya walking along the path towards the churchyard. Joe climbed gingerly to his feet.

"Hey, cuz!" she cried when she saw him. "I've been looking all over for you. What are you doing here? And what's happened to your face?"

Joe touched his sore cheek. His finger came away

covered in soot. He hesitated, unsure what to say. He didn't know his cousin that well. He felt sure she'd laugh at him if he started telling her he'd just been back in time to the Battle of Britain. After all, she'd spent most of the past three days laughing at him for his strange country ways. That was when she wasn't completely ignoring him.

Joe had been sent to stay with Maya and her dad, Uncle Theo, here in Slade Common in south-east London. His parents thought it would do him good to spend some time with his relatives, instead of idling away his summer holiday reading detective stories at home in Dorset.

"It'll be fun!" his mum had assured him. "Your Uncle Theo's a historian, and you like history, don't you, Joe?"

That much was true. Uncle Theo *was* a historian, and Joe *did* like history. But what his mum hadn't told him was that Uncle Theo would be so busy writing his history books that he'd have hardly any time for Joe.

That meant Joe was forced to spend all his time with Maya.

She was Joe's age, but about as different from him as it was possible to be. Where Joe was quiet and polite, she was loud and rude. And she was *always* on the phone or texting her friends. She had about a hundred thousand of them, or so it seemed.

Joe could count his own friends on the fingers of one hand. He preferred books to people, if he was honest. And the books he loved most were detective stories. He'd read so many, he reckoned he could solve any crime.

One day he'd be a famous detective. All he needed was a mystery to make his name – a mystery worthy of his talents.

As for Maya, he doubted she had time for mysteries. All she ever read were her friends' text messages.

She'd been on the phone just now in fact. She and Joe had been walking along the high street when Sarah (or was it Serena or Samantha or Susannah?) had called her. Bored with waiting for the conversation to end, Joe had wandered into the churchyard. He'd been standing by an overgrown grave when he'd spotted it, in the undergrowth at the foot of the gravestone – a smartphone. Joe had picked it up. The phone was bound to have the owner's details somewhere in it. He could return it to the owner himself – and perhaps get a reward.

So imagine his surprise when he'd switched it on and read this:

Hello Joe Smallwood.
Which time would you like to visit?

Joe had been struck dumb. How could a phone he'd just found possibly know his name? He'd never been to this place before. At least the question had seemed innocent enough – at first. Joe had assumed it would take him to a history website.

Beneath the question were some wheels that you could spin with your fingers: one wheel for the date, one for the month and one for the year. He'd spun the wheels to 18th August 1940, expecting to be given some facts about what had happened on that date in history.

Next thing he knew, a loud drone was filling his ears and a German warplane was hurtling through the sky towards him!

The phone had actually sent him back in time.

If you would like to order this book, visit the ReadZone website: www.readzonebooks.com

FICTI●N EXPRESS

The Time Detectives:
The Mystery of Maddie Musgrove
by Alex Woolf

When Joe Smallwood goes to stay with his Uncle Theo
and cousin Maya life seems dull, until he finds a strange
smartphone nestling beside a gravestone. The phone
enables Joe and Maya to become time-travelling detectives
and takes them on an exciting adventure back to Victorian
times. Can they prove maidservant Maddie Musgrove's
innocence? Can they save her from the gallows?

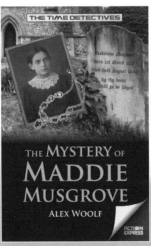

ISBN 978-1-783-22459-3

Drama Club
by Marie-Louise Jensen

A group of friends are involved in their local youth drama club at a small city theatre. When their leader, the charismatic Mr Beaven, announces he wants to put on a major new play at the end of the summer holidays, the cast is very excited.

Amidst rivalry, hopes and disappointments, will there be more drama on or off the stage?

ISBN 978-1-783-22457-9

FICTI●N EXPRESS

The School for Supervillains
by Louie Stowell

Mandrake DeVille is heading to St Luthor's School for Supervillains, where a single act of kindness lands you in the detention pit, and only lying, cheating bullies get top marks. On paper, Mandrake's a model student: her parents are billionaire supervillains, and she has superpowers. The trouble is, Mandrake secretly wants to save the world, not destroy it.

THE SCHOOL FOR SUPERVILLAINS
LOUIE STOWELL

SAINT LUTHOR'S

FICTI●N EXPRESS

ISBN 978-1-783-22460-9

About the Author

Alex Woolf was born in London in 1964. He played drums in a teen band, and, in his 20s, he rode his motorbike and travelled in America (where he nearly ended up as a barracuda's lunch!). In between, he did lots of dull and dangerous jobs. His worst job was washing up in a restaurant kitchen full of cockroaches!

Finally, he settled down to write books. Alex has written non-fiction books on subjects like sharks, robots and the Black Death, but his greatest love is writing fiction, and he claims to have been writing stories almost since he was able to hold a pen.

His books for Fiction Express include *The Mystery of Maddie Musgrove* (the first title in his Time Detectives series) and *Mind Swap*, a story in which a bully and his victim change places. He has also written *Chronosphere*, a science fiction trilogy about a world in which time moves super-slow, and *Aldo Moon and the Ghost of Gravewood Hall*, a story about a teenage Victorian detective who investigates ghosts in a spooky old mansion.